D1467018

A Shaun the Sheep MOVIE

FARMAGEDDON ™

OFFICIAL BOOK OF THE FILM

Sweet Cherry

Sweet Cherry Publishing Limited
Unit 36, Vulcan House,
Vulcan Road,
Leicester, LE5 3EF
United Kingdom

Published in 2019

2 4 6 8 10 9 7 5 3 1

ISBN: 978-1-78226-587-0

Written by Gemma Barder
Edited by Cecilia Bennett

Printed and manufactured in China
C.WM004

CLOSE ENCOUNTERS
OF THE HERD KIND!

CHAPTER 1

A gentle breeze passed through the sleepy town of Mossington. It was a quiet night. Some might say *too* quiet. Two snails were slowly making their way down the street, when the street light suddenly flickered above them. They looked up. In a nearby shop window TV screens went blank, and then something unknown streaked across the sky.

Farmer John and his dog, Bingo, had just emerged from the Forest Takeaway. Their only concern? Getting home before their delicious parcel of hot fish and chips went cold.

Friday night was fish and chip night. Always had been. Always would be. Nothing got in the way of fish and chip Friday. Not the Friday Farmer John's cows escaped and devoured the floral displays in Mossington Town centre; not the Friday his wife inconveniently gave birth to his daughter, and certainly not the Friday everyone else in Mossington was watching the World Cup final.

So, it was no surprise that Farmer John didn't notice the strange streak of lights that shot across the sky that evening. Unfortunately for the farmer, his dog Bingo definitely did notice them. With a howl, Bingo ran off into Mossington Forest, following the lights at breakneck speed. Farmer John followed with his chips still firmly wedged under his arm.

Inside the forest, the moonlight cast eerie shadows through the trees. Farmer John moved quickly, his eyes darting from left to right. He'd never been in the forest at night before and he was starting to worry. Mostly he was worried that his chips were getting cold, but he also had a strange feeling that someone was watching him. Before he had time to finish that thought, Farmer John

spotted Bingo on a high ridge. He scrambled up and was just about to give his wayward pooch a telling off when ...

Light.

The brightest, blindingly white light you could imagine, filled Farmer John's eyes.

Ker-thunk! The Farmer squinted, trying to work out what was making that strange, loud, clunking sound.

As his eyes adjusted to the light, Farmer John found that he could just make out the edges of a figure. At first he thought it was one of the kids from town, but as he

looked harder he could see that whatever the figure was, it certainly wasn't human. In fact, it didn't look like anything he had ever seen before.

Farmer John had had enough. He grabbed Bingo's lead and made a run for it, spilling his chips over the forest floor as he ran. All he had wanted that evening was a quiet stroll followed by fish and chips. Now he was running for his life through Mossington Forest – and even worse, his chips were gone.

As Farmer John's footsteps faded into the distance, the ghostly figure gave up trying to catch up with him. It had seen something far more interesting. But what did the creature want? What was it doing there? And *why* was it now devouring Farmer John's chips from the forest floor?!

When you live on Mossy Bottom farm you
have two options:

    1. Do as Bitzer tells you, eat grass and
            live a boring life.

                OR

    2. Break the rules and have a little bit
            of fun!

For Shaun the Sheep and the rest of his
flock, there was no question. This was a

group of sheep who simply loved having fun and making mischief. At the top of today's list of activities? Frisbee!

Shaun picked up the Frisbee and got ready for his turn. He was a playful sheep whose cheekiness often got him into trouble. He loved hanging out with the Flock, especially Timmy who basically thought Shaun was the coolest sheep in the field. Shaun loved this (who wouldn't?) and tried to impress Timmy whenever he had the chance.

Today, Shaun decided it was time to show Timmy what he could really do with a Frisbee.

He pulled his arm back, then threw the disc as high and as fast as he possibly could.

The Frisbee sailed up into the air, across the field, past Timmy, and over the hedge. The sheep watched in dismay as it whizzed through the sky and landed straight in the crunching, twisting wheels of the Farmer's combine harvester. It didn't stay there for long. With a loud clunk, the combine harvester spat the Frisbee back out again at top speed, right in Bitzer's direction.

Bitzer. If there was one animal on the farm who actually knew what was going on from day to day, it was Bitzer the sheepdog. He loved to make up rules, and Shaun had a theory that he was trying to eliminate fun from the farm entirely. Today Bitzer was happily cleaning a window. Out of the corner of his eye, he noticed something move. He turned around and – *WHAM!* Bitzer narrowed his eyes at Shaun as he removed the Frisbee from his mouth.

Shaun looked hopefully at Bitzer, maybe he'd see the funny side of things? But no. Bitzer stormed over to the sheep's field, whipped out his tool kit, and hammered a 'No Frisbees' sign into the grass. Then he turned to carry on with his many jobs around the farm.

Shaun sighed. He liked Bitzer, they had known each other for a long time after all. But he couldn't understand why Bitzer was so against having fun. More often than not, Bitzer and Shaun were at opposing ends of an argument. Shaun shrugged his woolly shoulders. It was far too nice a day to give up. Shaun wanted fun, and there were plenty of places on the farm for fun to be found. He rounded up the Flock and had a think. Frisbee was off the table, so what was next?

First, they tried to play on the Farmer's combine harvester.

Then they did a BMX jump.

15

Then they tried a hot air balloon ride.

After the Flock tried to shoot Nuts out of a cannon, Bitzer finally had enough. He barked angrily at the unruly Flock and rounded them up into the barn. Maybe an early bedtime would convince the sheep to behave.

Shaun and the Flock were locked up for the night in the barn with nothing but a bag of sheep nuts for company. The thing is, sheep nuts aren't very tasty. Have you ever tried them? Shaun certainly had.

16

Faced with a long night with nothing to eat but sheep nuts, he knew he had to come up with something else. Something genius. Something cunning. Something delicious.

Later that evening, Bitzer began his nightly patrol of the farm. In Bitzer's experience, it was always best to make sure that all was well before he settled down for bed. If there was a problem, fixing it was Bitzer's responsibility. You could never be sure if a fox was on the prowl, or if a fence had blown down, or if Shaun was having a secret moonlight football game with the pigs. But that had been on Wednesday (Shaun and the Flock had beaten the Pigs 25 – 0), tonight was a different story.

The useful thing about Bitzer was that he was very predictable. When Shaun knew Bitzer would be checking the fence at the very far edge of the farm, the Flock loaded Shaun onto a see-saw they had made. They dropped the bag of sheep nuts on the other end. Shaun flew up into the air and out through the barn window. Like a fleecy ninja, Shaun rolled through the dog flap in the Farmer's front door and sneeked past the living room. He crept into the kitchen where he knew the Farmer's computer would be laying open on the counter.

Shaun rubbed his hooves together. A couple of clicks later, Shaun was on the Forest Takeaway website. He ordered a stack of pizzas to be delivered immediately. Goodbye sheep nuts, hello steaming hot pizza!

CHAPTER
3

Dexter, The Forest Takeaway delivery boy thought he had met just about everyone in Mossington. There was Mr and Mrs Pocket, who ordered one sausage supper on a Tuesday night to share in front of their favourite TV show. Horace Chomp, the school's headmaster, who asked for his pizzas to come with extra garlic and anchovies, which made his breath extra-smelly for all the children he taught the next day. Then there was the Lowther Family, who liked their fish and chips *on top* of a cheese and tomato pizza.

So it came as quite a surprise when Dexter was asked to deliver a stack of pizzas to an odd-looking and rather wobbly gentleman who seemed to have moved into Mossy Bottom Farm. The man seemed to have three wooden legs and was wearing a coat and gloves, despite being inside the cosy farmhouse. He said nothing as he took the pizzas and quickly shut the door.

Dexter looked at his hand to examine his tip of old football coins and buttons. He sighed and hoped that the customer wouldn't become a regular.

Inside the farmhouse, Shaun shrugged off the Farmer's coat, jumped down off the three-legged stool and popped the gloves back in the basket by the front door. His mouth watered as he grabbed the pizza boxes and headed back to the barn. He arrived to a chorus of cheers from the rest of the Flock.

But their joy wouldn't last for long. You see, one of the things about sheepdogs is that they have an excellent sense of smell. And, as well as being able to sniff out trouble, Bitzer was *excellent* at sniffing out a pizza.

Especially when the pizza was somewhere it shouldn't be.

Bitzer marched in behind Shaun, took the pizza boxes off the distraught sheep, and headed back to the farmhouse. He knew the Farmer loved pizza. For once, the Flock's mischief would make Bitzer look good!

Sure enough, at the sight of the pizza boxes, the Farmer jumped up from his chair. What a good idea! They grabbed a box each and lifted the lids ... only to find that the pizza boxes were empty!

Back in the barn, Shaun opened the one pizza box he'd managed to hide from Bitzer. The Flock crowded around expectantly. It, too, was empty.

This left two options: either Dexter had become peckish on his way to Mossy Bottom Farm and decided to eat all of the pizzas in one go, or someone else had stolen the pizzas when no one was looking.

Shaun and the Flock headed to bed with grumbling tummies. Shaun wasn't sure if it was his stomach, or something else that was keeping him awake that night. He tossed and turned and couldn't fall asleep. Eventually Shaun got up and stared out of the barn window from his spot high up in the barn. He watched as a line of strange vehicles rumbled along the road into Mossington. Big black vans and cars with shining headlamps. Out of the corner of his eye, Shaun thought he saw something move among the crops. A closer look revealed ...

Nothing.

It must have been a rabbit, or the wind. With a yawn, Shaun slowly made his way back to bed. Somehow he couldn't shift the feeling that someone, or something, was watching him.

Early the next morning, Bitzer finally opened up the barn. A famished Flock hurtled past him to the feeding trough. Thanks to his sleepless night, Shaun was slow to get up. He stretched and slowly followed his friends to their disappointing breakfast. By the time Shaun had arrived at the trough, there was nothing but a few crumbs left.

Shaun wandered off glumly. After the trouble he'd gone to the previous night, what did he have to show for it? Nothing. The Flock couldn't even be bothered to save him any food. Just as Shaun started to think he might

never eat again, he spotted a pizza crust on the ground. It was better than nothing. He reached for it and went to put it in his mouth. Before he could, Shaun spotted another crust a little way off. Then another. And another ...

The trail of pizza crusts led all the way back to the barn. Shaun followed it. He wanted to know who had taken the pizza from the night before. He was also secretly quite impressed that anyone could eat as much pizza as him in one sitting.

The barn should have been empty. The Flock had disappeared to the field, to follow up their breakfast with the Farmer's finest grass. Streams of sunlight filtered through the beams, casting shadows here and there. Suddenly, Shaun saw a shadowy figure dart across the room. Then he heard a clatter. It came from behind the stairs at the back of the barn. He tried to ignore the trembling in his knees as he edged closer.

CHAPTER 4

Shaun peered into the shadows. He could make out a small figure. It wasn't a sheep, or a rogue pig, or one of the Farmer's naughty nieces or nephews on their yearly visit. This creature was not like anything Shaun had ever seen before. As the figure moved into the light, Shaun could see that she had big eyes and long, floppy pink ears. She was also blue. Blue! Shaun had never met anyone blue.

'ARGH!!!' screamed Shaun.

'ARGH!!!' the creature screamed back at him.

Shaun dived behind a haybale. After a couple of seconds, he slowly peaked over it. The creature smiled shyly back at him. Well, she didn't *look* dangerous. The sheep cautiously tossed a bit of pizza over to the creature. She reached out and gobbled it up. Shaun held out another piece to coax the little thing out of her corner.

Whatever this little creature was, she wasn't scary. Shaun gave her an encouraging smile, and she took a few steps towards him. She muttered some strange sounds that made Shaun giggle with surprise.

The creature giggled back in a perfect imitation. Shaun grinned, but then his jaw dropped in shock. The creature was actually glowing!

Just then, the creature looked through the door and noticed the Flock outside. Feeling less frightened now that she had met Shaun, she dashed out to meet more friends.

The Flock had seen many strange things at Mossy Bottom Farm, but they had never met anyone like this. The odd little thing was copying all the sounds they made! Shaun followed her out and introduced the creature to his friends.

The creature seemed to be trying to tell them something. She went from sheep

to sheep muttering urgently, but politely, in her little language. Once they got over her strangeness, they began to realise just how adorable she was. They liked her even more when she revealed how great she was at impressions.

Having picked up the Farmer's mail and newspaper from the mail box as he did every morning, Bitzer passed the Flock who were suddenly being very well-behaved. In Bitzer's world, there was nothing more suspicious than a group of sheep acting normally. He padded closer to the Flock and

sniffed the air. He growled a warning to the sheep, and was surprised when someone in the Flock growled back at him. As Bitzer looked around, Shaun growled again to clear his throat, then smiled. The sheep were certainly behaving oddly, but they did seem to be behaving. The puzzled pooch trotted off again.

The Flock had managed to keep their new friend safely hidden. As Shaun waved goodbye to Bitzer, he couldn't help but notice the front page of the newspaper he was holding.

So that was it! The creature was an alien! Shaun looked over at his new friend. He had a feeling she had a lot to tell him if he only knew how to talk to her.

CHAPTER
5

Lu-La was lost. Hopelessly lost on a planet she had never been to before. To Lu-La, Mossy Bottom Farm was full of weird and wonderful things. There were the plump, pink creatures who seemed to like swimming in ... umm ... whatever the brown stuff was that they were swimming in. There was the cross-looking yellow creature wearing an interesting blue hat. And there were her new woolly friends,

who seemed to like eating more than anything else. In this unfamiliar landscape, there was one thing that Lu-La thought she recognised. It was large, made of metal, and looked pretty powerful. So they had spaceships here, too! Lu-La made her way over to it, marvelling at her lucky find.

Before anyone knew it, Lu-La had jumped excitedly into the combine harvester's front seat. Shaun followed her with a smile. This sweet little alien was so curious! He sat in the driver's seat and tried to show her how the combine harvester worked.

Meanwhile, Lu-La was trying to tell Shaun about her plan to fly this strange 'spaceship' back to her home planet. The only problem? Shaun didn't understand a word of what she was saying.

Lu-La closed her eyes and concentrated. Her floppy ears gently rose into the air and started to vibrate. The ignition key turned. Shaun jumped as he heard the engine roar into life. Lu-La was controlling the combine harvester with her alien powers!

The machine sped off over the fields, churning up crops as it careered around in circles. Shaun grabbed the steering wheel, he had to admit this was good fun!

Lu-La looked disappointed. Why wasn't this spaceship taking off? Earth spaceships seemed a lot harder to control. She concentrated harder. The levers controlling the combine harvester moved frantically in all directions.

Shaun and Lu-La zoomed around the field. As they passed the other farm animals, Lu-La's powers sent them hovering into the air, creating a floating cloud of pigs and chickens over the machine.

In the shade of the farmhouse, Bitzer was admiring a freshly painted batch of signs. He sighed happily as he sipped on a cup of tea. He had to admit that the morning was going quite well.

All of a sudden, the combine harvester rounded the corner. Bitzer watched, open-mouthed as it showered him and his tea with scattered crops, and ... surely that wasn't the Pigs flying around after it? There was nothing Bitzer could do to stop the combine from mounting a pile of ramp-shaped wood. He watched in horror as it came crashing down, sputtering and rolling to a stop.

Shaun breathed a sigh of relief as the pigs and chickens rained down around the combine harvester. Lu-La looked disappointed. Maybe this big metal machine wasn't a spaceship after all?

Shaun was suddenly aware of Bitzer scowling at him through the window. It was time to make a speedy exit. Shaun grabbed the little alien's hand and ran. Bitzer grabbed the keys from the ignition. When he looked up again, Shaun was gone.

But Bitzer had bigger things to worry about. He wasn't the only one who had noticed the chaotic joy ride around the farm. The Farmer was angrily stamping through the field towards him. Bitzer braced himself. He knew how much the

Farmer loved his combine harvester. He was a combine harvester enthusiast. While most people dream of a bigger house, an exotic holiday or a flashy new car, the Farmer had always dreamed of owning the WHEATCHOPPER 500. A top-of-the-range, shiny, super-powerful, *mega* combine harvester that would make him the envy of all the farmers in Mossington.

But that was only a dream. For now, the Farmer cared lovingly for the combine harvester he had. The combine harvester that had crash-landed right in the middle of his field, and that was currently surrounded by mangled parts.

Bitzer held his breath and waited for the Farmer to erupt with rage.

All remained quiet. The Farmer stood and stared at the crops in the field. Bitzer looked at him in concern. Was he ok? Was this the final straw? The Farmer stood stock still. The look on his face navigated its way through rage to confusion, and on to outright joy.

Uh oh. Bitzer knew his master well enough to know what this look meant: the Farmer had had an idea! Bitzer couldn't be sure what it was, but he had a horrible feeling it was going to mean more work for him.

Standing among the strange patterns the combine harvester had carved out in the crops, the uneasy dog waited for his master to say something.

CHAPTER
6

Although Lu-La's new friends were very friendly, they weren't that smart. They clearly didn't understand a word of what she was saying even though she was speaking perfectly clearly. As she shuffled back into the barn, Lu-La grabbed a stick from the floor. She started to sketch out a detailed diagram of her home planet in the dust on the barn floor.

Shaun stared over his new friend's shoulder in total bafflement. The drawing seemed to be important to the little alien, but it just looked like shapes and squiggles to him. He wished he knew what she was trying to tell him. The confused sheep shrugged and shook his head.

Lu-La tossed the stick to one side. She'd had an idea. She needed something more ... dynamic. Wiggling her long ears again, Lu-La started to do the same thing that had sent the combine harvester into overdrive. Shaun looked nervously about him. This time Lu-La was making various fruit, vegetables, eggs, and random objects levitate. They came to a bobbing halt above her head.

Lu-La was making a solar system. More specifically, she was making *her* solar system, out of anything she could find around the farm that looked vaguely like the planets she knew so well.

Now that she had the planets in place, Lu-La levitated a toilet seat, a hubcap from the Farmer's beaten up old car, and a jam jar lid from Bitzer's recycling pile. She put them all together to make a model of what looked very much to Shaun like a spaceship. Lu-La flew the spaceship away from the solar system, and crash landed it on the barn floor next to a symbol she had drawn in the dirt. The small alien pointed enthusiastically at the spaceship, and motioned for Shaun to take a look.

Now he understood. Lu-La needed to find her ship and go home. But where was it? Shaun studied the symbol and jumped up excitedly. Of course! He knew the symbol very well. Just like Mr and Mrs Pocket, Horace Chomp, the Lowther Family, and Farmer John did. He ran off, and came back holding a menu for the Forest Takeaway. At the top was the very same symbol. Finally! Lu-La and Shaun jumped up and down, excited that they had understood each other at last.

After they had finished jumping, Shaun looked at Lu-La thoughtfully. He had only met her that morning, but Shaun knew he had to try to help this little alien get back

home. Secretly, he couldn't help thinking that such a task was bound to come with a huge side-order of adventure! Life at Mossy Bottom Farm had been a bit boring recently, what with Bitzer's determination to ban anything fun. This was exactly what Shaun and the Flock needed.

They had to come up with a plan. The Flock were all eager to pitch in. They decided they would make a fake Shaun to put in the field. That way Bitzer and the Farmer wouldn't realise that Shaun was missing. They found an old rocking horse and covered it in spare wool. Shaun took a good look at the Flock's creation, then gave it a thumbs up. Of course, it wasn't as good-looking as the real thing, but it would do the trick!

Shaun and Lu-La tiptoed out of the barn to the far end of the farm, narrowly dodging Bitzer along the way.

Once they reached the wall, they had a new problem. It was too tall for either of them to climb over! Shaun looked around desperately, then his eyes fell upon one of Bitzer's many signs. He could feel an idea brewing ...

After a few minutes, Shaun had used the signs to build a little staircase up the wall and out of the field. He clambered over, then turned to offer a hand to Lu-La. Lu-La? Where was she? Suddenly, the baffled sheep heard a sound behind him. There she was! Shaun giggled. There was so much more to Lu-La than he ever imagined.

Shaun unfolded the Forest Takeaway menu and showed Lu-La the little map on it. Lu-La and Shaun looked at each other. This was going to be a piece of cake.

Meanwhile, Shaun and Lu-La weren't the

only ones interested in the Forest Takeaway. Thanks to Farmer John's sighting, the takeaway and forest next to it, were crawling with members of the Ministry of Alien Detection. A group of people in yellow boiler suits darted here and there, taking readings with devices, and talking to each other in muffled voices. The workers' massive suits meant that no one could really tell which one they were talking to, so everyone just called them the Hazmats. The person in charge of this gang of top-secret workers was a tall, stern-looking figure. Agent Red.

Agent Red was known at the Ministry of Alien Detection as one of the toughest, most hard-working, alien-obsessed agents

the ministry had ever known. She spent her whole life thinking about capturing aliens. She thought about aliens all the time, she even dreamt about them. No one knew that something had happened to Agent Red a long, long time ago. Something she was determined to put right. They just knew that she was the hardest worker the Ministry had.

As Agent Red strode along, MUGG-IN5 followed closely behind her. The sophisticated, top-of-the-range robot had been issued to Agent Red to help with her

investigations. MUGG-IN5 was programmed to help Agent Red with anything she required – and he was more than happy to do it. He handed Agent Red a file. She raised an eyebrow. Now, this was *interesting.*

Agent Red and the Hazmats followed Farmer John, the local man she had been interviewing, through the forest of the sleepy little town she had been called to. She had seen it all: from a local *sure* they had seen a UFO in the sky ... which turned out to be the neighbour's kid's new remote-controlled helicopter. To the woman who'd *definitely* just had a conversation with an alien ... which turned out to be her nephew dressed up for a comic book convention.

This time, something was different though. Agent Red could smell it in the air, and it wasn't just the smell of old chip fat coming from the local takeaway. Farmer John climbed a steep ridge and pointed into the clearing below.

There was nothing there.

The Hazmats quickly surrounded the confused farmer and led him away from the scene. Usually this would be where Agent Red's investigation stopped. She would pack up her clipboard and climb back into her surveillance van. Not this time. Agent Red stared off into the distance. Something was happening in Mossington, she just couldn't be sure what, yet.

CHAPTER

7

Shaun was realising that Lu-La was no ordinary alien. In fact, Lu-La was one of the cheekiest, most fun-loving friends he had ever had! She saw opportunities for fun everywhere. It was just like having an excitable alien twin! They'd made popcorn in the corn field, been chased by a dog, and had a go on someone's trampoline.

As they came out from the old railway

tunnel, Shaun spotted a bike leaning up against an old yellow dumpster. He looked at Lu-La – was she thinking the same thing he was?

Shaun and Lu-La clambered into the dumpster. This would make the perfect transport for a lost alien and a fugitive sheep! With a wave of Lu-La's ears, the two friends began thundering down the road. After a few wrong turns, the pair finally made it into Mossington Town.

Shaun tentatively peeked out under the dumpster's lid. He looked around the streets in wonder. The news of Farmer John's alien encounter had turned Mossington into a centre for UFO enthusiasts. People dressed

in robot costumes chatted happily as they walked down the street. A coachload of alien fans had just arrived, and they were busy getting their cameras ready for a sighting.

Shaun gulped.

If any of these people spotted Lu-La the game would be over. He would never get her back to her ship. She would be taken away, questioned, photographed and who knows what else? Shaun was going to have to keep a close eye on Lu-La. He reached out for her, but grasped air instead ... Where was she?

Lu-La's eyes widened. She was drawn

towards the window of Milliways Supermarket. She had never seen such a display of earthling treats! The doors of the supermarket swooshed open, and she gasped in delight. It looked just like the door on her spaceship!

Shaun rushed up to the supermarket window just in time to spot Lu-La filling her arms with groceries. He tapped at the window and desperately beckoned to Lu-La. He needed to get her to come back outside so he could hide her away as soon as possible. Lu-La looked at him, then took a massive bite out of the toilet roll she was holding.

Shaun rolled his eyes and sneeked past the security guard, into the supermarket. He ran from aisle to aisle until, finally, he spotted the mischievous alien in the frozen food section. He got to Lu-La just as her tongue got stuck to a frozen pizza. Shaun yanked it free and the pizza went flying through the air, slicing the top off a lady's hairdo as it went!

Lu-La was confused. The last time she had eaten pizza it was steaming hot and delicious! Before she could get to the bottom of the mystery, Lu-La spotted the sweet aisle. It glowed in a cacophony of neon colours and the smell was something

Lu-La had never experienced before. She couldn't help herself. Lu-La used her many arms to grab as many sweets as possible from the supermarket shelves and shovelled them into her mouth. She glowed all sorts of different colours as she ate. After happily munching for a few moments, Lu-La started to feel a bit funny ...

Shaun braced himself as he watched Lu-La's ears waggle. Something told him that introducing Lu-La to more sugar than he could eat in a week wasn't going to end well. The little alien took off like a tornado. She darted around the supermarket, sending food flying off the shelves and forcing shoppers to dive for cover.

Suddenly Lu-La screeched to a halt. An odd look crept across her face, and she let out the loudest sound Shaun had ever heard in his life! The almighty burp sent the supermarket shelves toppling over like dominoes.

Making the most of the chaos, Shaun and Lu-La quickly left the shop. They jumped back in their dumpster before the supermarket's security guard could make any sense of what had just happened.

Unfortunately, someone *had* noticed Lu-La. Not far from Mossington, in a top-secret underground base, one of Agent

Red's Hazmats had picked up Lu-La's enormous burp on one of the alien-detection recorders. The Hazmat jumped up and ripped the report from the printer. For once, Agent Red would be pleased.

The Agent's bright red lips curled into a satisfied smile as her eyes darted across the readings. Agent Red was right. She'd *known* something was going on in Mossington, and this was all the proof she needed.

CHAPTER

8

The Farmer was still in shock. He'd planned everything. A whole theme park and a spectacular show. Farmageddon was the biggest, most ambitious idea he'd ever had in his life! Where on earth had all this inspiration come from? Usually the Farmer only ever had his farm on the brain. There was so much to keep on top of: feeding the animals, harvesting the crops,

A Shaun the Sheep MOVIE
FARMAGEDDON ™

Farmer John and Bingo
encounter a spaceship!

No more Frisbees on Mossy Bottom Farm!

Shaun discovers Lu-La hiding
in the barn.

Lu-La is an instant hit with the flock!

The damaged field gives the Farmer an idea ...

Shaun realises that Lu-La last saw her
spaceship near the pizza takeaway.

Lu-La and Shaun escape the farm
to go find her spaceship!

Agent Red investigates the site of
Farmer John's alien encounter.

Lu-La is just as adventurous as Shaun!

The Farmer shows the Farmageddon plans to Bitzer.

Lu-La discovers sweets.

The Flock start building the
Farmageddon theme park.

Bitzer spots Shaun and gets his leg stuck in
a bucket trying to chase him.

Hurrah! Shaun helps Lu-La find her spaceship.

They try to start the ship.
Something's missing! Will they find
the fob so Lu-La can go home?

saving up for a WHEATCHOPPER 500 ... Now was not the time to get distracted. He pulled out his blueprint.

Bitzer stood in the kitchen of the farmhouse staring down at the blueprint the Farmer had just rolled out in front of him.

Inspired by the news reports about a nearby alien sighting, when he'd seen the crashed combine harvester, the Farmer hadn't seen a mess of destruction and ruined crops: he'd seen an *opportunity*. The trail that the combine harvester had cut looked just like the crop circles he'd read about! He was going to turn his field into the sight of a genuine alien encounter, complete with

rides and a theatre show re-enacting the night with the Farmer in the starring role. It would earn him all the money he could want, and it was going to be called:

FARMAGEDDON!

Not only was Bitzer put in charge of the construction of the park and stage, he had also been given an extremely tight astronaut's outfit to wear while he advertised the Farmageddon theme park around town. Bitzer ignored the stifled giggles from the Flock as he handed out hard hats and building materials to the confused sheep.

Bitzer would never get this theme park built all by himself, he needed all the help he could get! After barking some instructions and throwing the blueprint at the sheep, Bitzer walked into town to hand out flyers and put up posters. The Farmer wanted to make sure that every alien buff and UFO spotter in town knew about his new project.

As Bitzer glued a flyer to a lamp post outside the Forest Takeaway, something familiar caught his eye. Someone that looked just like Shaun was running into Mossington Forest! What was that naughty sheep up to now?

In a moment of outrage, Bitzer stumbled backwards and landed one paw in the bucket of glue. He shook his leg, to no avail. But that wasn't going to stop him. Bitzer ran into the forest, the bucket stuck on his leg making him waddle and clank as he picked up speed. Shaun wasn't going to get away with messing around this time! Not when everyone else was hard at work. The displeased dog picked up Shaun's scent and, with his nose firmly on the ground, began tracking the sheep's steps.

Blissfully unaware that Bitzer was tracking

them, not to mention Agent Red, MUGG-IN5 and the Hazmats, Shaun and Lu-La were finally getting closer to Lu-La's ship.

Lu-La squealed with joy as they climbed the very same ridge where Farmer John had been with Agent Red just a few hours earlier. Just like Agent Red, Shaun only saw a wide, open space where the spaceship should have been. Shaun scratched his head in disappointment. Perhaps the other aliens had taken the ship and left Lu-La behind? He sighed and turned to comfort Lu-La. To Shaun's confusion, the alien gave him a cheerful hug and happily ran into the centre of the clearing. A second later, she disappeared.

Shaun was dumbstruck. His jaw dropped as the air in the clearing shimmered and a gleaming spacecraft appeared before his eyes. Lu-La's ship had been invisible all this time! Shaun was impressed. Wherever Lu-La came from, they made far more impressive machines to ride around in than the Farmer's combine harvester. Lu-La stood in the doorway and gestured for Shaun to come in.

Shaun tentatively stepped onto the ship. He couldn't believe he was actually inside an alien spacecraft! He followed Lu-La to the

cockpit. The hard work was over now. Lu-La could fly home, but not before Shaun had had a good look around first, of course.

Meanwhile, in her underground base, Agent Red had hacked into Mossington's CCTV circuit. She was desperately searching for any sign of alien activity. Any trace of the creature that had produced those intergalactic soundwaves her equipment had picked up earlier.

But what was this?! It was blurry, but its outline didn't match the usual mix of arms and legs that made up most of the residents of Mossington. There! She zoomed in on a strange, silver, lolloping creature heading speedily into Mossington Forest – the exact place where Farmer John had said he'd spotted the spaceship. Surely this was the alien she had been searching for all along! Or perhaps it was a rather blurry image of a dog with a bucket on its leg ...

Bitzer hadn't looked up for a good ten minutes. He trusted his nose would take him where he needed to go: to Shaun and a jolly good telling off. For now, nothing else mattered. It was just him and the scent.

As Bitzer took another big deep sniff, he hit his head against something hard. Something that jammed his helmet over his head. He stood up. He was no longer in the forest – he was inside some kind of machine! He scrabbled around frantically, accidentally pressing some strange buttons next to the door he had collided with. Without warning, the panicked pooch was sucked up into the ceiling. Soothed by an alien lullaby, by the time he arrived in the cryo-pod, Bitzer had been sent into a deep, floating space sleep.

CHAPTER 9

Shaun jumped into the pilot's seat of Lu-La's spaceship and pretended to be flying deep in outer space. The Flock had once made a pretend spaceship out of hay bales, but it was nothing like this. To name but a few differences, there were fewer buttons and a lot more straw ...

Lu-La started pushing buttons. The ship roared into action. Shaun gulped – was he ready for an adventure into deep space? Before he could answer that question, the ship juddered to a stop. Shaun was so relieved that, at first, he didn't notice Lu-La's panic-stricken face. She was looking for something. Something important. As Lu-La rummaged around, Shaun's eyes fell upon a framed picture of Lu-La with two older-looking aliens. Lu-La was standing between them clutching a little alien teddy. He was hit by a sudden realisation. Lu-La was a little child!

Suddenly everything made sense! No wonder she liked the sweet aisle at the supermarket. A wave of pity washed over the sheep's face: this meant his little alien

friend probably had no idea how to fly this spaceship home.

As Lu-La noticed Shaun looking at her with sadness and confusion, she decided it was time to tell him how she had crash landed on Earth. Slowly she reached up to her friend's head and used her telepathic alien powers to reveal the story to Shaun.

Just like hundreds of small children back on Earth, Lu-La liked to wake up much earlier than her parents. Lu-La was definitely a morning person, and she

had a lot of energy! She tried to wake up her parents, but they just rolled over and went back to sleep. Lu-La looked around her home for something fun to do.

She'd built an alien den the day before, and she was bored of beating her friends at burp wars.

Lu-La spotted the key fob to her family's spaceship on the table. She prodded it. Outside, the ship appeared on the driveway. Lu-La squealed and ran outside. She could play space explorers inside the cockpit! As she played, Lu-La accidentally knocked the fob into its slot. Before she knew it, the ship came to life and started hurtling towards Earth.

Lu-La was terrified. This wasn't meant to happen!

The spaceship came crashing to a stop. Shakily, Lu-La made it to the door only to realise that she was somewhere completely unfamiliar. She noticed a movement in the trees. Still clutching the key fob, she wandered over to Farmer John to ask for help. He ran off with a yell, spilling his chips as he went.

Shaun looked from Lu-La to the spaceship's complicated control deck. Did Lu-La expect him to drive the spaceship back to her home planet? Before he had a chance to answer, the spaceship started to shake from side to side. A loud clanging sound came from outside. The spaceship began to move ...

CHAPTER
10

Agent Red smiled triumphantly. She had tracked the strange, metal-footed alien all the way back to the very place she had visited that morning. She watched as it entered the spacecraft. She had wasted little time in calling for backup. It arrived in the shape of a huge lifting vehicle and a giant tarpaulin, big enough to cover a football pitch. With the spaceship safely covered,

MUGG-IN5 and the Hazmats transported the ship to Agent Red's underground base.

A little way away, one of the Hazmats discovered something strange. An unusual key fob was hidden under a pile of leaves not far from Farmer John's discarded chips. She picked it up and dropped it into an evidence bag.

When the ship finally came to a stop, Lu-La and Shaun peeked nervously out of the window. It had been a bumpy ride, and only now did they dare look out at their new surroundings. They were in what looked like a massive underground base. Shaun noticed a small robot feeling its way around the ship, looking for a way in. He glanced at Lu-La, and put a finger to her lips. They waited in tense silence until MUGG-IN5 finally wheeled away, unsuccessful.

The two friends peered out of the spaceship again. With a gasp, Lu-La noticed something that made her big eyes grow even larger. One of Agent Red's Hazmat's was holding the fob. Lu-La looked desperately at Shaun. One of the people who had just transported her ship to this strange cave was holding *her* fob!

If one of the Hazmats worked out what the alien technology could do, it wouldn't be long before they were all inside the ship, and all hope of Lu-La getting home would be lost. As they watched, the Hazmat made her way over to Agent Red and handed her the fob. The agent's eyes lit up as she grabbed it, and hurried away to her office.

Shaun had to think fast. Luckily, he was used to doing this on the farm. He had lost count of the number of times he and the Flock had avoided a good telling off from Bitzer by quickly covering up whatever mischief they had been up to. The other skill Shaun had learnt was how to get around the farm undetected. He was about to use both of those skills to help Lu-La and escape.

Shaun signalled to Lu-La to stay where she was, then he carefully unscrewed a panel in the spaceship floor. He dropped down into the underground base just as MUGG-IN5 and the Hazmats started taking selfies in

front of the ship. Shaun couldn't blame them, he was just thinking how he'd love a picture to take home to the Flock. They were *never* going to believe what he had been through today.

Shaun followed Agent Red to her office and watched as she whistled a secret tune to unlock the door. As Agent Red disappeared inside, Shaun started to think the mission was hopeless ... if only there was a way to imitate that sound.

Lu-La had ignored Shaun's instructions to stay put in the ship's cockpit. Catching up

with him, she copied Agent Red's whistle to perfection, opening the door in the process. Shaun slipped inside and hid behind a coat stand. Agent Red was staring at an old, scruffy-looking child's drawing. As he glanced around the room, Shaun spotted the fob sitting on the agent's desk. This was going to take careful manoeuvring!

Finally, Shaun reached the desk and went to grab the fob. It wasn't there! He looked up. Lu-La was using her powers to levitate the fob. Shaun stared at it in horror. Of course, Lu-La thought she was helping, but Shaun knew that if anyone here saw a levitating piece of alien equipment floating around the office, they would be in deep, deep trouble.

Shaun locked eyes with the alien and gestured for her to stop. Lu-La abruptly lost her concentration. Before Shaun could catch it, the fob clattered to the floor. As it bounced, the fob activated the spaceship's engines, sending the Hazmats running around the underground base in a panic, and waking Bitzer from his deep space sleep ...

CHAPTER 11

Bitzer blinked, and looked around blearily. No, this must be a dream. He closed his eyes again.

WHACK!

Bitzer woke up again to something hitting him in the face. What was going on? He never napped while he was on farm business. He wondered how he had found his way back to the farm when he thought he had been

chasing Shaun through Mossington Forest. It must have been a dream. Water suddenly sprayed out from the wall at him. It was followed by a blast of warm air. By the time a brush appeared at mouth level, Bitzer was gradually realising that he didn't actually know where he was. He stumbled along wondering why his leg felt so heavy. It was awfully foggy in here too ... he needed some fresh air. Was that a door he could see?

Clouds of dry ice billowed from the door of the spaceship. In the doorway stood a strange alien figure. The Hazmats hid behind

their desks, as it made its way slowly down the landing ramp.

Bitzer couldn't see a thing. He waved away the clouds of dry ice. As they dissipated, to his surprise, he saw a group of people wearing hazmat suits staring back at him.

A nervous Hazmat walked up to Bitzer, who stared back utterly confused. Who were they? Where was he?

Agent Red was perplexed: the fob was nowhere to be seen. Suddenly, a commotion drew Agent Red over to the window. From her office, she could see the strange yellow alien!

As the agent desperately shouted instructions to the Hazmats, Shaun grabbed the fob and Lu-La, and dashed back to the ship.

Bitzer didn't really know what was going on, but there were two things he was sure of:

1. He definitely shouldn't be here.

2. Neither should Shaun!

Bitzer had barely registered the sheep's presence, when something far more concerning caught his attention: a tall woman in a smart suit, wearing a crazed expression, was bringing an ominous-looking cage right towards him. What they wanted with a sheepdog when they had alien technology to deal with was beyond him, but he wasn't about to argue. Bitzer ran, followed by the Hazmats.

After a long and hectic chase, Bitzer was finally cornered. One of the Hazmats slowly advanced towards him, backing him closer to the open cage. But instead of pushing Bitzer into the cage, the Hazmat moved straight past it, towards the landing ramp.

The other Hazmats were confused. This wasn't the plan. What was this person doing? He looked a bit different to the rest of them too. Agent Red scowled as she noticed something woolly poking out of the Hazmat suit. It was Shaun! He gestured at Bitzer and they legged it into the spaceship, locking the door securely behind them.

CHAPTER
12.

Bitzer had a lot to wrap his head around. He was on an alien spaceship, but it was better than being outside of it and being chased by those strangers in yellow suits. Shaun wasn't supposed to be here either, but he couldn't be cross with him as he was pretty sure Shaun had just saved him from something far worse.

Then, Bitzer noticed who Shaun was with.

Bitzer stared at Lu-La. Lu-La stared back at him. Bitzer shrieked – he was face to face with a genuine alien! Lu-La shrieked back in a perfect impression of Bitzer.

Shaun didn't have time to explain everything to Bitzer. He had the fob and it was time to get out of here. Shaun put the fob into the slot on his dashboard. It fitted perfectly! He pressed the buttons on the control pad at random: one of them was bound to get the ship moving. Sure enough, the ship started up.

Agent Red ran to the other side of the underground base. *Not so fast*, she thought as she pulled a big lever. Up above her, the roof began to close over the escaping

spacecraft. The spaceship sped up and made it through, not a moment too soon. Agent Red's face fell as the roof slammed shut.

Bitzer, Shaun and Lu-La were frozen in terror as the ship sped through the countryside, leaving nothing but chaos in its wake. The ship abruptly changed direction. Bitzer and Shaun exchanged a worried look … they were in space!

It was even more of a shock for the little robot attached to the outside of the spaceship. MUGG-IN5 had still been searching for a way inside the ship when

they left, and was now firmly attached to the ship's hull. He continued to listen into the ship with his stethoscope.

As they moved away from Earth, the spaceship suddenly stabilised. All three passengers looked at each other as the autopilot sign pinged on inside the cockpit. They were safe, for now, and the spaceship was chartering a course for home ... Lu-La squeaked in delight – she was finally going home!

Bitzer shook his head. This had gone too far. He was about to be sent through space to an alien planet. He couldn't let that happen, he had to get back to the farm! What about the Farmer? The Flock? The Farmageddon theme park was opening soon!

To Bitzer all this alien was, was a trouble-maker and the reason he was now speeding away from Earth at light speed. Lu-La knew what she had to do next. She took Bitzer's hand and showed him her story in the same way she had shown it to Shaun. She *needed* to go home. She was far too little to be away from her own planet. Shaun shrugged at Bitzer. He knew it was a crazy plan, but what choice did they have?

As Bitzer opened his eyes, he groaned with understanding. Even he knew that returning a young alien to her family was more important than completing the Farmer's latest hare-brained scheme. The dog stood up. If they were going on a rescue mission, they were going to do it right. He flipped through the instruction booklet for the spaceship's control panel.

Lu-La was giddy with happiness. In a few hours she would be back home with her family! She looked at Shaun. For the first time since meeting him, Lu-La was the one who knew her surroundings and Shaun was completely clueless. She decided to show Shaun one of the coolest bits of kit on the ship, something she was 100 per cent sure he would love – the catering orb!

The catering orb was amazing. All you had to do was push buttons until something you wanted to eat appeared. To Shaun's surprise, they had a slice of earthling pizza on offer! Before he could select it, a yellow paw reached out to stop him. Bitzer gave Shaun a stern look and slapped a warning sign over the machine. As the dog went back to study the instructions, Shaun gave Lu-La a mischievous wink. He wasn't going to let a sign get in the way! He'd eaten nothing all day and here was pizza at the touch of a button!

But Shaun's grasp of the catering orb wasn't quite as advanced as Lu-La's. Soon hundreds of pizzas were flying out of the orb, and Shaun could do nothing to stop them. They whizzed through the air, hit the wall with a wet-sounding *thwap*, and landed in messy, cheesy heaps on the control panel. One of the pizzas hit a big button and the spaceship screeched to a halt. Autopilot had disengaged. Lu-La stopped giggling. This was bad. The ship performed a very tight turn. A message flashed up: they were returning to Earth. Lu-La cried out. She wanted to go home!

CHAPTER

13

The Flock were finally putting the finishing touches to the Farmageddon theme park, which now contained a huge tower and a ramshackle stage. The Farmer was finally ready for the world to see his very own re-enactment of the famous Mossington Alien Encounter. He was so busy getting everything ready for the first visitors that he didn't notice a real spaceship hurtling towards the farm.

Thunk! With each bounce, Lu-La's ship broke into smaller pieces. As parts landed in the cornfields, MUGG-IN5 was sent flying. Only the seats that Lu-La, Shaun and Bitzer were holding onto for dear life remained intact as they came to a final, juddering halt.

Shaun opened his eyes – he couldn't believe they were all alive! But his grin of relief soon turned to despair as he saw Lu-La's devastated face. How was she going to get home now?

Bitzer glared at Shaun. This was all his fault. If he hadn't messed around with the catering orb, Lu-La might be home by now. He wished that Shaun could be more

responsible and think about others before he did such silly things. Bitzer handed Lu-La her teddy, and placed a sympathetic arm around her shoulders.

Shaun felt terrible as he watched Lu-La moving miserably around the wreckage. He should have listened. Shaun had assumed that Bitzer just wanted to stop the Flock from having fun. Now he understood that the dog was just trying to keep them safe. Shaun sighed. He really had wanted to help Lu-La. And now because of him, there was no way she could get home.

He looked over at the little alien. Lu-La was desperately trying to reassemble the spaceship. But even if she had known how it was all meant to fit together, she was so upset that she couldn't summon up her powers at all.

As Lu-La and Bitzer headed back to the barn, Shaun sat among the wreckage feeling miserable. Just then, he heard a faint beeping sound coming from under one of the twisted pieces of metal. It was Lu-La's fob! It had survived the crash, and it was flashing. Shaun picked it up and stared at the blinking red light and little symbol that had appeared on it. The fob must be trying to send out some sort of signal. A signal to Lu-La's home planet!

The signal on the fob wasn't very strong – Shaun could see it needed to light up completely to work. Shaun thought about all the times the Farmer had been on his mobile phone. Whenever it wasn't working properly, he would walk around the farm with his arm high in the air. That was it! Shaun knew he had to get the fob up high. Really high. High enough to make contact with Lu-La's home planet. He needed help.

Meanwhile, the Farmer had just put the finishing touches on his Farmageddon theme park. He peeked out from the stage curtains, and spotted a large group of alien enthusiasts heading over. His first customers! There was just one more thing to do. He flipped a switch. With a crackle and a few worrying sparks, the park lit up!

Shaun turned at the noise and spotted the tower. That was it! The answer to all of Lu-La's problems! Shaun burst into the barn to find the Flock relaxing after a long day of building. Shaun quickly explained what had happened. As is always the way with good friends, the Flock wanted to do anything they could to help. They pulled out the

blueprints for Farmageddon and gathered around. It was time to come up with a plan.

A little while later Shaun stood in front of the Flock looking very proud of himself. It was simple, really. The flock had built a model spaceship that was meant to be lowered down from the tower onto the stage during the Farmer's performance. All the Flock had to do was attach a milk churn to the other side of the mechanism. As the spaceship was lowered down, Shaun would hop in the churn with the fob, and be hauled up to the top of the tower.

Some time later, Bitzer led Lu-La back to the barn. It was time to make the best of a bad situation, and show her to her new home. Bitzer frowned. Where were the Flock? Just then Lu-La pointed to something that had caught her eye. There in front of her was a blackboard, and on it there was a picture of her fob.

Shaun and the Flock sneeked into Farmageddon disguised as sci-fi fans and joined the crowd. Shaun hadn't seen Lu-La or Bitzer since the crash, but he didn't have time to look for them, he was intent on helping his friend. Despite the Flock's hard work, the Farmageddon theme park was distinctly underwhelming. Groups of very disappointed visitors wandered around the park. Eventually they settled into their seats in front of the stage, wondering what on earth they were about to witness.

As the Farmer prepared himself for his starring role in the play, in a makeshift dressing room at the back of the stage, the Flock helped Shaun to climb into the milk churn at the bottom of the tower. With a quick thumbs up, Shaun let them know he was ready. Before the Flock could winch him up, Shaun spotted Bitzer standing just a few feet away from him with a worried-looking Lu-La by his side. Usually this would be the end of Shaun's plans, but instead of telling Shaun to get out of the churn, Bitzer handed Shaun a hard hat. He knew that Shaun wanted to help Lu-La and make up for what had happened in the spaceship. And Bitzer wanted to help the little alien too. Beside him, Lu-La gave Shaun a shy high five.

CHAPTER
14

In a neat little house on a quiet, suburban street, a little girl was lying in bed. It was very late at night and something had woken her up. As she sat up and peered out of her bedroom window, the little girl was astounded to see two pink and blue creatures with large eyes and floppy ears on her garden lawn. Aliens! The creatures waved at the little girl, and she waved back with a big smile.

The next day at school, the little girl couldn't wait to tell everyone what she had seen. She even drew a picture to show to her classmates. But instead of being excited and amazed, the little girl's classmates laughed and pointed at her. It began with a small chuckle, but soon the whole classroom was laughing at her – even the teacher! The little girl flushed red. Tears pricked her eyes. Why didn't anyone believe her?

From that day on, the little girl vowed that one day she would prove that her story was true. No matter what it took.

Over 20 years later, Agent Red unfolded the drawing of the aliens outside her front garden that had started it all. She was on the verge of making her dream a reality.

Agent Red had followed the tracker on her trusty robot, MUGG-IN5. She stood among the wreckage of the ship that had, only a few hours before, been safely stowed in her own underground base. A faint whirring made Agent Red turn around. MUGG-IN5 was hobbling towards her, still slightly on fire from the crash. He pulled himself up into a salute. He was no use to the agent

now. Agent Red ignored the loyal robot and walked away. The alien she had come so close to capturing was nearby and she wasn't about to let it get away again. The agent reached into her pocket, pulled out a remote control, and pointed it at her surveillance van. She watched with a small smile as the van transformed into a deadly weapon. MUGG-IN5 sagged despondently. He'd braved the depths of space to please Agent Red, and she hadn't so much as thanked him.

Meanwhile, backstage, the Flock had begun to steadily hoist Shaun up the tower.

As they did so, the Farmageddon model spaceship was lowered in the opposite direction. So far, so good. The signal on the fob was getting stronger, but it still wasn't strong enough.

Shaun would have to go as high as the winch could carry him to activate the fob. But, what was this? He had stopped moving. Shaun glanced down to the stage, only to see the Farmer pull Bitzer onto the stage. It was time for him to play his part. This left Shaun swinging in the breeze, with no way to move up or down the tower. If only Shaun could reach out to the tower itself, perhaps he could climb the rest of the way to the top? He tried to swing himself over, but his arms just weren't long enough. Someone else's were though. Just then, Shaun saw a familiar pair of long, pink and blue, tentacle-like arms reaching towards him.

Lu-La! The little alien had bravely climbed up the tower to help. She grabbed onto the milk churn, and Shaun managed to clamber onto the tower. It was still a long way to the top, but it was Lu-La's only chance of making it home. Shaun took a deep breath. What would Bitzer do? He'd probably tell Lu-La to get back down on the ground where she was safe. Shaun knew his mischievous friend well enough to know that she would never agree to that. He gave Lu-La his hard hat, swung the little alien onto his hip,

and started to climb. Far below them, the curtains opened on the Farmer's play.

A loud, whirring, mechanical noise made Shaun, the Flock, Bitzer and the audience turn around. Agent Red was wearing a giant robotic suit made out of her black van. She looked like some kind of futuristic robot fighter. Some of the sci-fi fans were actually drooling with jealousy – what a costume! But Agent Red's suit was no costume. The headlights shone down on Bitzer as Agent Red recognised him. This was the alien she had spotted

in Mossington. The alien that had been at the base. The alien that had escaped!

With one long leap, Agent Red crashed onto the stage. The sci-fi fans sat up, the play had just become 100 per cent more interesting! Agent Red smashed the fake spaceship Bitzer was sitting in, and glared at him.

As Bitzer struggled to get free, his alien costume began to fall off. He barked angrily at Agent Red. The penny dropped. This creature wasn't an alien. He was a dog!

Agent Red could barely contain her fury. She had been tracking a dog all this time!

The audience started laughing beneath her. Her face flushed red. Angrily, she tossed Bitzer aside, sending him flying into a stack of equipment.

As she straightened up, Agent Red's mechanical eye focussed on something else. Something blue and pink climbing up a tall tower with what looked like a sheep. Something she *knew* was definitely an alien. She had seen creatures like her before, a very long time ago.

CHAPTER
15

Shaun and Lu-La reached the top of the Farmageddon tower. Suddenly it started to shake. Agent Red had leapt onto the tower beneath them and was quickly catching up to them. Desperate to help, the Flock followed her and tried to take her mechanical suit apart.

Shaun was too scared to look down. With a shaking hand, he held the fob up to the

sky as far as he could reach. Lu-La squealed with delight as a beam of light shot out of the top of the fob. It was sending a signal to her home planet! They had done it! They had finally found a way to get Lu-La home.

But Lu-La and Shaun's joy was short lived. Just a few feet below them, the scary-looking woman who had stolen Lu-La's ship earlier that day was climbing the tower in a terrifying robot suit. Shaun and Lu-La started to throw down parts of the big Farmageddon sign above them, but Agent Red wouldn't be stopped. She

was too powerful, and she had nothing to lose. Just as Agent Red was about to grab Lu-La, Shaun noticed something small and yellow flying through the air towards them. It was Bitzer!

Bitzer had found the cannon he had stopped Shaun from shooting Nuts out of not long ago. He had fired himself across the length of Mossy Bottom Farm. There was no way he was going to let some robot lady stop this sweet little alien from getting home to her family!

Bitzer smacked straight into Agent Red.

She lost her grip on the tower and fell fast in a heavy heap onto the stage. The audience broke out into applause. They all believed that what they were witnessing was part of the Farmer's show!

Agent Red might have been out of the way, but Shaun, Lu-La and Bitzer were in trouble. The tower was beginning to fall apart. The three friends looked at each other in terror. The next moment, they were falling. Bitzer and Shaun grabbed hold of Lu-La to protect her. They each closed their eyes as they waited to follow Agent Red to the ground ... but the fall didn't happen. Something was keeping them in mid-air. It was a huge beam of light. A beam of light from a spaceship!

As the spaceship gently deposited Lu-La, Shaun and Bitzer safely to the ground, the Flock gathered round to watch it slowly open. Out of a cloud of icy mist, came two creatures who looked just like Lu-La, but bigger. Their faces were filled with worry as they called out Lu-La's name. Shaun recognised them from the picture in Lu-La's spaceship. It was Lu-La's parents, Ub-Oo and Me-Ma!

Lu-La rushed into her parent's arms and the family gave each other a big, relieved hug. Lu-La gently tugged on Me-Ma's arm and dragged her over to say hello to Shaun. Lu-La's parents smiled and said something that Shaun was sure meant 'thank you'.

Shaun and Bitzer grinned at each other and breathed a sigh of relief. Everything seemed to have worked out perfectly.

Everything apart from the fact that Agent Red still wanted to catch her alien, that is!

Agent Red wasn't going to let Lu-La get away that easily. She rose from the stage in a tangle of metal and wires, determined to catch her alien before it got away. Without warning, her robot suit turned back into a van, trapping Agent Red inside. MUGG-IN5 rolled out from behind her. He had finally had enough of doing everything for Agent

Red without any thanks, so he decided to teach her a lesson.

Me-Ma couldn't help but stare at the strange lady who was causing all the commotion. She shuffled towards the van as Agent Red stopped shouting. Using her alien powers, Me-Ma opened the van door and touched Agent Red's head with one of her long, pink tentacles.

Agent Red relaxed. A large smile spread across her face. These were the aliens she had met as a child! She pulled her drawing out of her pocket and showed it to Me-Ma, who gave her a big alien hug. Agent Red held her phone out for a selfie. Now she could prove that everything she had seen as a little girl was real! And this collection of strangely intelligent farm animals, their clueless farmer and a bunch of sci-fi fans knew it too.

Now, all that was left was for Lu-La to say goodbye. Tears welled in her big eyes as Lu-La hugged Shaun and Bitzer and waved goodbye to the Flock. Then, Lu-La, Ub-Oo and Me-Ma boarded the spaceship. Moments later, the ship shot into the air. Soon it was just another bright star in the sky.

A moment of silence settled over Mossy Bottom Farm. Then the audience of sci-fi fans erupted in applause, they had never seen such a realistic show before! The Farmer was thrilled. He wasn't sure how it had happened, but his play was a roaring success.

A week later, things were back to normal on Mossy Bottom Farm. The Flock were enjoying their field, rather than building in it. The Farmer had just received his new WHEATCHOPPER 500 thanks to the success of the Farmageddon theme park, and Shaun was back to playing Frisbee. There was just one change. When Bitzer put up a sign, Shaun knew that it was because he didn't want the Flock to get hurt. And as long as

Shaun played by the rules and promised not to let the Flock get out of hand, Bitzer was more than happy to join in their Frisbee games. He rivalled Shaun with his elaborate, over-the-top throws, one of which had just sailed past Shaun and was heading straight for the Farmer's new combine harvester ...